Furry FRIENDS

Marshmallow Magic

HOLLY WEBB

Illustrated by Clare Elsom

SCHOLASTIC

For Nina, who is lucky enough to live in Paris!

Scholastic Children's Books
An imprint of Scholastic Ltd
Euston House, 24 Eversholt Street, London, NW1 1DB, UK
Registered office: Westfield Road, Southam, Warwickshire, CV47 0RA
SCHOLASTIC and associated logos are trademarks and/or
registered trademarks of Scholastic Inc.

First published in the UK by Scholastic Ltd, 2017

Text copyright © Holly Webb, 2017
Iluustration copyright © Clare Elsom, 2017

The right of Holly Webb to be identified as the author
of this work has been asserted by her

ISBN 978 1407 15433 6

A CIP catalogue record for this book
is available from the British Library.

Printed by CPI Group (UK) Ltd, Croydon, CR0 4YY
Papers used by Scholastic Children's Books are made
from wood grown in sustainable forests.

1 3 5 7 9 10 8 6 4 2

www.scholastic.co.uk

CHAPTER ONE

Sophie sat on the steps, gazing at the little tree. It looked a bit like an upside down ice cream cone, but apart from that, it was a perfectly usual sort of tree.

It didn't look like a guinea pig's front door, not at all.

And yet Sophie knew that it was. She

1

had seen a small ginger-and-white guinea
pig disappear inside it only two days
before. A ginger-and-white guinea pig
wearing a bright pink ballet skirt.

Now she was desperate to see Josephine again — but the gardens of the church of *Sacré Coeur* were full of children and tourists and photographers and everybody except for small ginger-and-white guinea pigs.

Sophie's brother Dan had got sick of waiting. He had sat with her for what he said was ages and ages, but was actually only five minutes, and then had gone off hunting serpents in the dusty bushes around the side of the slope instead.

Sophie peered round, trying to see him. Perhaps she should just go and join in? Their mum had met a friend and she was sitting chatting on one of the benches on the side paths, but soon she would say that it was time to go. They had only stopped for a little while on the way home from school because Sophie had begged and begged. She had told her mum that the steps leading up to the *Sacré Coeur* were her new favourite place. Mum had been surprised, but then she'd told Sophie that she loved them too, with the beautiful church at the top and the white stone of the steps gleaming in the sun. The grass was so green it almost glowed, she told Sophie, laughing. There was definitely something special about it.

Sophie had to squash her lips together

to stop herself telling Mum that the hill below *Sacré Coeur* had its own family of guinea pigs, living under the ground. They came out every night to nibble the grass neat and short and pick up anything that had been left behind. It was the guinea pig gardeners who made the green lawns so beautiful. Mum would never have believed such a silly story, though. Dan hadn't believed Sophie either, until he'd met them for himself.

"I should have brought Josephine another macaron," Sophie sighed to herself. "I'm sure she would have come out for a macaron. Especially if it was a lavender one."

"Actually, she wouldn't," said a small but very stern voice. It was a voice where all the words were perfect, with neat, clipped edges. It sounded rather cross. It certainly didn't sound like Josephine's giggly little squeak.

Sophie turned round, very slowly, and saw that there was a guinea pig standing beside her, wearing one of the little grass hats that Josephine had told her were for disguise if they had to pop outside. The guinea pigs were supposed to be a great secret – Sophie had only discovered that they were there when she had fallen off the wide stone edge of the steps and Josephine had come scurrying to help her.

All the guinea pigs that Sophie had ever seen – talking or not – had been plump and furry and cuddly. They had *not* looked disapproving. But this sleek white guinea pig was definitely glaring at her.

"It was you who gave it to her, wasn't it?" the guinea pig said, putting her paws where her hips would have been if she were human-shaped. "Do you know how silly that was? It was quite irresponsible." She said the long word rather

carefully, rolling it around her mouth as though she enjoyed it.

"I'm ever so sorry," Sophie whispered. She had bought Josephine one of her favourite lavender macarons with her pocket money, to say thank you for helping her with a mean girl at school. It sounded as though Josephine had eaten all of it in one go. "I didn't know it was wrong to give guinea pigs macarons. . ."

"Of course it is! We live on grass and hay and seeds! Green leafy vegetables! Not sweet treats like macarons! Josephine is bedridden!" the white guinea pig hissed importantly.

"I am not!"

Josephine squeezed out of the small hole under the tree and trotted over to Sophie. She didn't look as though she'd been ill in bed, although perhaps her round black eyes weren't quite as sparkly as before. She was still wearing her bright pink ballet skirt – it flounced out around her middle and shimmered as she hurried across the grass.

"I'm so sorry," Sophie told her guiltily. "I didn't know that it would make you sick."

Josephine patted Sophie's foot gently. "Don't worry, it didn't. Oh, it's true that

I was slightly too full of macaron to go out nibbling grass that night, but that was all."

"You said you didn't want to see another macaron again in your life and that purple was your least favourite colour ever," the white guinea pig pointed out crossly.

"This is my sister, Angelique." Josephine took hold of the white guinea pig's paw and the pair of

them made an elegant bow to Sophie.

Sophie bowed her head back at them, trying not to giggle.

"She's very serious," Josephine whispered.

"I can hear you!" Angelique snapped.

"Well, you are." Josephine turned to Sophie. "She worries too much. About everything. But that's actually quite useful, because then she comes up with brilliant inventions to help. Like these grassy hats. Angelique thought of them and now we all wear them if we have to come outside in the daytime."

Sophie looked round at Angelique,

wanting to tell her that she thought the hats were very clever, but the white guinea pig was gazing down at the grass and the fur around her nose had gone a pale shade of pink.

"She's shy as well," Josephine put in helpfully and Angelique let out an embarrassed squeak.

"No, I'm not!" Then she glanced sideways at Sophie, her dark eyes glittering crossly.

Sophie chewed her bottom lip. She wasn't sure why, but she had a feeling that Angelique didn't like her. She'd only just met the little white guinea pig, though. How could Angelique decide not to like her all at once?

Maybe it was that she was nervous about meeting new people? Sophie felt like that sometimes. She had been too shy to speak to anyone at her new Paris school for weeks.

"I really like your hat idea," she said, smiling at Angelique. "How did you think of it?"

"I just did," Angelique said coldly, and she glared at Sophie again.

Sophie gulped. There was no mistaking it – Angelique wasn't just shy, she was being mean. And she was so small and furry and sweet-looking that her meanness seemed much worse. Even

Josephine turned round and glared at her.

"Why are you being unkind to Sophie?" she demanded. "You shouldn't talk to her like that. She's my friend."

Angelique's nose quivered and went

even pinker and Sophie gasped as she suddenly understood. The other guinea pig was *jealous*. Sophie was the first child that any of their family had spoken to. None of them had made a human friend before. Angelique was used to having her funny little sister all to herself.

Sophie sighed, very, very quietly. What was she going to do? She didn't want to make Angelique sad, but she couldn't go away and pretend that she'd never met the guinea pigs – Josephine was her friend. Somehow, she would have to make Angelique like her.

Chapter Two

Sophie eyed the two guinea pigs, wondering what to do. How could she persuade Angelique not to be jealous?

Josephine seemed to see that Angelique was sad as well. She caught her sister's paw and waltzed her on to the balustrade where Sophie was sitting. She twirled about, her little pink paws skittering on the stone, trying to get Angelique to dance with her.

But the white guinea pig dug her claws into the stone and yanked her paw away, refusing to join in.

"Stop it, Josephine!" she squeaked and folded her paws over her plump white tummy. "You're being silly! Someone will see you!"

Josephine stopped for a moment, glancing around at the visitors who were huffing and puffing their way up the steps. Then she began to twirl again. "I don't think they will," she gasped. "They're all looking at the church. I don't think anyone's going to notice us. And the sun makes me want to dance!" She pointed her feet and hopped up and down, flouncing out her pink tutu.

"Well, it doesn't make me want to!" And Angelique sat down huffily on the edge of the stone balustrade. "It's too hot and I don't like being out here. We should be safely hidden away inside the burrow."

"Don't you like dancing?" Sophie asked. She'd been trying very hard to think of something to say to Angelique, but she looked so grumpy it was hard to talk to her.

"No. Not all girls have to, you know." She glared at Sophie. "I suppose *you* do?"

Sophie nodded. "Yes. I go to ballet. I'm not very good at it, though. I fell over last week when we were supposed to be balancing on one foot." She stood and tried to show Angelique what she meant, stretching out her foot in front of her and wiggling it.

Angelique's nose crinkled, as though she wanted to laugh, but couldn't quite let herself. Sophie smiled at her. "It was funny, sort of. After I stopped feeling stupid."

Josephine was still dancing, spinning round and round, and holding out her pink paws to the sunshine.

"She's a very good dancer." Angelique watched her sister enviously. "I fall over too, sometimes. I trip over my own feet when I'm thinking about other things. How can she whirl round and around like that without getting dizzy?"

"Maybe she *is* dizzy and she just doesn't mind?" Sophie suggested, watching Josephine spin. She was going so fast that her ginger fur and her white fur had turned into one peachy-coloured blur, with a streak of shocking pink round the middle.

"That's not at all sensible," Angelique said primly, but Sophie smiled again, thinking how happy Josephine looked.

"Why are you smiling like that?" Angelique asked, and her voice sounded sharp and cross once more. "There's no need to smirk. Not everyone needs to be able to dance, you know! I do other things."

"Oh, I know you do!" Sophie nodded eagerly.

"You know far too much. Josephine shouldn't have told you our secrets." Angelique sniffed. "She shouldn't even have shown herself. It was very unwise. I told everyone so."

I'm sure you did, thought Sophie, with a tiny sigh.

Josephine had stopped twirling in the sunshine and now she was tottering towards them, swaying and giggling. "Oh, Sophie, Angelique, I'm so dizzy! Hold me up!"

Sophie laughed and stretched out her cupped hands so that Josephine could collapse into them like an armchair.

"You shouldn't let that girl do that," Angelique said, scurrying closer. "You wouldn't let her, if you'd heard what she just said."

"What?" Sophie blinked, confused.

"She was so horrible," Angelique hissed

to her sister, and she sneaked a mean
little sideways glance at Sophie. "She said
that you were a terrible dancer – that
you weren't the right shape for dancing
at all. *And* she said that your pink tutu

looks dreadful with your ginger fur. And no one who's ginger should ever wear pink."

"I didn't!" Sophie looked between Angelique and Josephine, her face shocked. How could Angelique tell such lies? Surely Josephine wouldn't believe her. Would she?

But the little ginger-and-white guinea pig was staring up at her in horror. As Sophie watched, she patted her pink ballet skirt, holding it out with her claws, looking at it – and then back at Sophie.

"I didn't say that, Josephine." Sophie looked at Angelique, shaking her head. "Tell her – please, tell her it's not true."

Angelique smirked, her expression so like one of the nasty, bullying girls at school that Sophie gasped.

"I am so sad, Sophie," Josephine said, her voice tiny, hardly even a squeak. She seemed to have got smaller, her gorgeous furry fatness had gone down like a leaking balloon. Then she turned away from them both and, as she walked back to the door under the ice cream cone tree, she wriggled out of her tutu, stepping through it and picking it up in her paw. She trailed it along behind her to her burrow, so that it gathered dust in all its pink flounces.

"Josephine, no! Come back, please!"

Sophie leaped up, wanting to run after the little guinea pig, to catch her in her arms and hug her tight, to make her believe it wasn't true, that she would never say such things. But as she scrambled to get there, Josephine was already disappearing through the little wooden door at the bottom of the tree and it swung tight shut behind her.

"What did you do that for?" Sophie asked Angelique. "Were you trying to make her sad? I can't understand why you'd be so horrible."

"Well, then, you aren't very clever, are you?" Angelique said. Her voice was sharp, but she wouldn't look at Sophie. She was staring down at the stone steps, as though she didn't want to meet Sophie's eyes.

Sophie caught her breath. "You're doing it to stop us being friends! You can't bear for Josephine to have a friend! Are you really that selfish?"

"I'm not selfish!" Angelique snapped. "I'm sensible. Guinea pigs and girls can't be friends." She said it in a know-it-all sort of tone, but Sophie could see that she didn't even believe that herself. Under her white fur she was blushing – she was completely pink, all round her nose and her paws. She was ashamed of herself.

"Sophie! Dan! Time to go!" Sophie

looked around, hearing her mum calling, and Angelique ducked down, pulling at her grass hat, scared that she would be seen,

"I won't let you do this!" Sophie whispered, as she got up to go and join her mum. "I'll keep coming here. I'll make Josephine listen to me, I'll tell her it wasn't true."

"I am her sister!" Angelique hissed back. "I know what's right for Josephine. You should go away and never come back!"

"I won't do that!" Sophie called, as she hurried down the steps. "Never, ever, ever! Just you wait and see!"

"There you are. Come on, Dan!"
Sophie's mum called. "We need to get
home. You've got all that work to do on
your history project, remember?"

Dan sighed and grumbled and

complained that Sophie never had any homework, but Sophie wasn't even listening to him. She was looking up the steps at the cross little white face that was still staring down at her.

Chapter Three

Sophie wriggled and twisted and turned over in bed, muttering into her pillow. Something was happening – something important. She sat straight up in bed with a gasp as she remembered. Josephine – and Angelique. Sophie clenched her fists, her nails digging into her palms, as she thought of the white guinea pig and her cruel, sneaky behaviour. The memory of Josephine's hunched shoulders and sagging fur floated in front of Sophie in the darkness and she felt her eyes burn with tears. Poor Josephine – she had looked so sad.

Then she jumped, startled by a strange noise outside her window. A tapping, scratching sort of noise. Sophie pressed herself back against her pillows, staring fearfully into the black night. It sounded as though someone was standing on her little balcony – and they were trying to get in...

But now that she thought about it, the tapping was coming from very low down on the tall glass doors. Whoever it was out there, they had to be very small indeed. Sophie squeaked delightedly and flung off her duvet, bouncing out of bed and across to the windows. She opened the curtains and pushed her nose up next to the glass, peering through. On the other side, a small furry figure was doing the same. Two pink, star-like paws were pressed against the windowpane and a little ginger-and-white face was gazing worriedly into hers. As soon as Josephine saw that it was Sophie, she

began to dance up and down, squeaking
so loudly that Sophie could hear her
through the glass.

"Josephine!" Sophie fought with the
catch, eventually pushing the glass door
open and hugging the little guinea pig

tight. "I'm so glad to see you! I thought you were never going to talk to me again. You looked so upset — oh, Josephine, you know that I never said it, don't you? Please say that you believe me."

Josephine let out a squeak of outrage. "My sister, Sophie, I am *furious* with her. How could she tell such lies? I am ashamed, I tell you, utterly ashamed that she should behave in such a way!" She shook her head and made a sound that was almost like a growl. Then she pressed her chilly apricot nose lovingly against Sophie's cheek. "But what makes it worse, Sophie, dear heart, is that she made me believe that you could say something like that. I should have known that you never would. Never. I was curled up in the burrow, thinking about it, and the more I thought, the sillier it sounded. I began to see that Angelique must have been making it up." She clenched her pink paws crossly. "I went and found her. I *made* her tell me. She admitted that it wasn't true."

"I don't really understand why she did it," Sophie murmured. "But I think perhaps she was a bit jealous. She's always been your special friend. . ."

"And she always will be!" Josephine

broke in impatiently. "She is my sister, after all. That doesn't mean that I can't be friends with you. Angelique is too selfish." She heaved a huge sigh, leaning against Sophie's knee. "What am I going to do about her? I'm so cross I don't ever want to speak to her again."

"The thing is, if none of you guinea pigs have ever spoken to a human before, it must have been very strange for her," Sophie said slowly. "She isn't used to you having anyone else."

"Maybe," Josephine muttered. "It isn't up to her who I talk to, though, or who my friends are! She can't tell me off!

And besides, she's always telling me to leave her alone. She says I'm too loud and she can't think with me dancing about."

Sophie sighed. "Dan does that to me too," she agreed. "It's very annoying. He only wants me around when there's no one better. If his friends come over, he acts like I'm just his annoying sister. It's horrible being the youngest."

"Oh, it *is*," Josephine said. "Everyone thinks I'm just a silly little squeaker who couldn't possibly be right about anything." She stretched one paw up to pat it against Sophie's hand. "You and I, Sophie, we are very alike, I think.

Although perhaps I am just a little bit of a better dancer. It doesn't matter. What matters is that we will always be friends, whatever Angelique says. She is my sister, but you are my *chère amie*. My very, very best friend."

CHAPTER FOUR

Sophie's mother looked at her and Dan worriedly. "You're sure? You promise you'll be careful? Dan, you won't let Sophie run into the road?"

"Mum!" Sophie glared at her. "You know I wouldn't! Dan's more likely to run into the road than me!" She swallowed as Dan twitched his eyebrows at her. She supposed it wasn't the most sensible thing to say, when they were trying to persuade Mum that they were grown-up enough to go to *Sacré Coeur* by themselves. She had begged Dan to come with her – she wanted to see Josephine again so much. That strange night-time meeting on the balcony had felt almost like a dream when Sophie woke up. She wanted to go and hug the little ginger-and-white guinea pig in the daylight.

"Well, I suppose I do have to finish this article," their mother murmured. "I know it's not very exciting for you, me having to work on a Sunday. And it is only just down the road. Take my phone, so you can call me if anything goes wrong."

Sophie nodded eagerly and Dan tucked the phone into his jeans pocket. They raced down the stairs of the big old house and out into the sunny street.

When they got to *Place Saint-Pierre*, Dan dashed up the steps and into the gardens straight away, but Sophie couldn't help stopping by the gate and gazing at the glittering white church so far above her. The carousel was turning and the music made her want to dance, just like Josephine. She felt as though all her

excitement and happiness was going to spill over. Her feet were almost dancing as she hurried up the first flight of steps from the street and along the curving path that led into the gardens. She had felt like this ever since Josephine had arrived in her bedroom – ever since she'd realized that the guinea pig must have climbed two floors up the twisting wisteria vine to reach her balcony. The thought made Sophie shudder, even though Josephine promised her it had been easy – so easy that even Sophie could do it. The guinea pig had cared *that much* about making up with her. It made something inside Sophie's tummy glow with happiness – when she wasn't feeling queasy about the climbing.

She darted on to the steps, looking hopefully for Josephine and wondering if she had talked to Angelique yet. Were the two guinea pigs friends again?

As it turned out, it was Angelique that she saw first. Sophie was hurrying up the steps behind a group of elderly ladies – who weren't hurrying at all, so that Sophie was hopping up and down with impatience behind them – when she saw a piece of crumpled paper lying on the grass. She was just thinking how unusual it was, since *Sacré Coeur*'s guinea pig gardeners never left any rubbish lying around, when she realized that it wasn't paper at all. It was a white guinea pig, curled up all of a heap. She was out there on the grass, without even her special hat. Something was terribly wrong.

"Oh, Angelique," Sophie whispered, and the white guinea pig lifted her head to look at her. Her eyes were always pinkish round the rims anyway, but now they looked scarlet.

"Angelique, are you all right?" Sophie asked anxiously, crouching beside her.

Angelique glared at her for a moment, her dark eyes glittering with fury. Then her shoulders slumped and she shook her

head. "No," she muttered. "Josephine says
she's ashamed to be my sister."

"Oh ... I don't think she means it,"
Sophie assured her. "She's just cross.
She'll change her mind."

"Will she?" Angelique whispered. "She

won't even talk to me. I've *never* known Josephine not to talk."

Sophie tried to hide her smile. She hadn't either. Even when Josephine was trying to be a super-secret agent at Sophie's school, she couldn't keep her mouth shut. Then her smile faded. She'd been furious with Angelique the day before, but now her miserable face was making Sophie feel just the teensiest bit guilty. After all, this was because of her.

"I'm sorry," she whispered. "I'll talk to her."

A loud hiss behind her made Sophie suddenly turn round. "Sophie! You should not be talking to that – that..." Josephine gave a prim little sniff. "I do not know what to call her without being rude."

"But, Josephine, she's your sister," Sophie gasped. "You can't say things like that."

"Yes, I can," Josephine muttered sulkily. "I never expected *you* to stand up for her, Sophie."

"Sisters do argue with each other. And brothers." Sophie looked around for Dan, wondering where'd he'd got to. He was supposed to be helping her look for the guinea pigs. She rolled her eyes a little as she saw him at the top of the steps by the fountain – he was messing around and splashing the water with a couple of his friends from school. "Look." She pointed at him. "Dan's up there. He promised me he was going to help me find you, but he's gone off to hang around with his mates from school. That's just what I mean."

Josephine peered at him and then looked at Sophie, her nose twitching suspiciously. "I don't understand."

Sophie sighed. "I don't think I'm explaining it very well. What I mean is, even though he's a bit useless sometimes, he's still my brother. And I love him! He was supposed to help me look for you and he's forgotten, but that doesn't stop me loving him. It's the same with you and Angelique. Sisters will always love you, whatever you do – oh, look. Dan's coming back down."

Dan had stomped away from the other two boys. Even from the bottom of the steps, Sophie could see that he was scowling horribly. Something was clearly wrong.

CHAPTER FIVE

Sophie and the two guinea pigs peered worriedly up at Dan. He was slouching down the steps with his hands in his pockets, still frowning.

"Is he coming here?" Angelique asked nervously. She stood up, as though she wanted to dart back into the burrow.

"Don't worry," Sophie said. "Josephine's met Dan before. He won't tell anyone about you. Dan's nice, most of the time. Although I have to say, he doesn't look very happy right now."

"Hello, Dan!" Josephine waved happily to him, but her face fell as he came closer. "He looks very grumpy," she whispered to Sophie.

"Hello," Dan muttered, slumping next to Sophie. Then he looked curiously at Angelique. "Hello."

"This is Josephine's sister, Angelique," Sophie explained, darting worried glances at the three of them. Angelique was upset, Josephine was cross, and Dan looked so sulky...

Angelique stared at Dan, her dark eyes panicky.

"Be nicer!" Sophie nudged Dan. Then, to Sophie's surprise, Angelique came a little closer and laid a paw on Dan's bare leg.

He twitched a little and grinned at her. "That tickles."

But Sophie noticed that the grin didn't really last. She was about to ask Dan what was wrong, when Angelique scurried into his lap and looked up at him. "Why are you so sad? Even your feet sounded unhappy."

"There are some boys from my
school over there." Dan pointed up the
hill towards the fountain, where the
other two boys from his class were still
splashing.

Angelique ducked, worried that they
would see her, but Dan shook his head.

"They won't notice you, don't worry."
He sounded miserable.

"Did you have an argument?" Sophie
asked.

Dan shrugged. "We were all just having
fun," he said. "Then Luc started telling
me about his project. You know that
history project we were supposed to do?"

"Ohhh..." Sophie had heard a lot
about the project a few weeks before.
Dan had told her that his teacher was
mad on history and wanted all their
projects to be *magnifique*. That was
the French for magnificent – Dan had
been a bit worried that his wouldn't be
magnifique enough.

"His dad's helping him build a model of some enormous castle out of sugar cubes! Luc's dad runs a café; they have *loads* of sugar cubes. What have we got?"

Sophie nodded understandingly. Their mum was a translator and their dad worked for a travel company. Neither of them were expert model-builders, and Dad was in Spain at the moment, anyway.

"What's Albert doing?"

"Drawing bits of some special cave paintings. He's really good at art. They both kept asking what I'm doing and if I was nearly finished, and then because I didn't know what to say — well, I sort of might have told them that I was making something totally amazing and it was a secret and they'd have to wait and see..." He pulled up a handful of grass and threw it on to the steps. Both Angelique and Josephine sucked in a horrified breath at the mess.

"Sorry!" Dan leaned over to pick up all the bits of grass, but Josephine scurried around tidying them before he'd got more than a couple. "I just don't know what to do. I haven't got anything amazing. I started trying to make a drawing of the Eiffel Tower. I've been working on it for weeks, but it looks like some weird alien. I hate being stupid."

"You aren't," Angelique pointed out.
"You can speak English *and* French very
well. How can you be stupid?"

"I know that really." Dan shrugged.
"But my project's going to be awful.
Especially when all the others are so
brilliant."

"There must be something
we can do," Angelique
muttered, clenching her
paws into tiny pink fists.

"I can't think what,"
Dan said. "But it's nice that
you want to help."

He ran his hand gently over her smooth white fur and Angelique wriggled in surprise — she wasn't used to being petted. But then she rubbed her face against his hand for a moment and looked up at him.

"Whenever I can't think what to do, I sit down and read a book. It always helps."

"You have books in your burrow?" Dan asked, sounding surprised.

"Not many." Angelique sighed. "Only the books that people leave behind by mistake. And most of the ones we have, there are bits missing. We have to chew the edges, you see, to make the books fit through the doors. And it always seems to be the most important words that get eaten." She smiled shyly at Dan. "But the newspapers, I can roll those up and squash them in. I *love* newspapers."

"Yes, they're very comfortable to sleep on," Josephine agreed. "Once they're nicely chewed up."

"That isn't what I mean at all! Sometimes..." Angelique dropped her voice to a whisper and the others leaned closer to hear. "Sometimes, I've come out of the burrow in the evening, just as it's starting to get dark, and I sit underneath a bench and watch someone reading. All I want to do is ask them if it's a good book or what they think of the news in their paper. It's so hard to pretend that I'm not there."

"That's really sad," Sophie whispered, and Dan ran a sympathetic finger over Angelique's little silky ears.

Josephine looked shocked. "Angelique! We aren't supposed to have anything to do with humans! You spent hours telling me off for talking to Sophie!"

"Well, I've never actually done it!" Angelique pointed out. "Not like you!"

"I could lend you some of my favourite books," Dan suggested. "I could find some thin ones, I'm sure. And then we could talk about them."

"Really?" Angelique stared up at him, her eyes sparkling. "Actual books?"

"I'll go home and look," Dan promised.

"That's all very well," Josephine said sternly, poking Dan's leg with her paw.

"But what are we going to do about your homework, hmmm?"

"Nothing." Dan let out a huge sigh. "We should go home, Sophie. I have to hand it in tomorrow. I suppose I should at least try and finish my drawing."

"*Hmf.* No." Angelique stood up and folded her arms. "We are not having this. We shall just have to make sure that your project is the best in the class."

"But I can't," Dan started to explain. "Mum hates making stuff and Dad's away, and I can't even think of anything cool to do. Everyone else has got their parents helping..."

"Yes, but you have me. Us," Angelique added quickly, when Josephine sniffed.

"Actually, I'm not very clever at making things either," Josephine admitted. "But I did like the sound of the sugar cubes. I'm sure I'd be good at *that*."

"You aren't allowed to eat them," Sophie said, giggling.

"And then what is the point?" Josephine threw her paws in the air and rolled her eyes in a very dramatic way.

Angelique frowned. "Hmm. Are you allowed to make *anything*?"

"Anything to do with the history of France. Monsieur Carle really likes the

Romans, though. I was trying to think
of something Roman to do, but dressing
up in a sheet and saying it's a toga isn't
going to be good enough. Not with
everyone else making sugar castles..."
Dan sighed again.

"I have it!" Angelique leaped off Dan's
lap and started to do a little victory
dance, waggling
her elbows and
swinging her bottom,
while the others
stared at her.
Angelique didn't
do dancing – she'd said
so herself.

"This is what happens when you offer to give her books," Josephine said to Dan, looking shocked. "She *never* dances!"

Angelique stopped and stood there, panting a little. "A catapult! A model catapult!"

"Like the ones the Romans used to invade France!" Dan nodded eagerly. Then he frowned. "I know what one looks like, but I'm not sure I could make it."

"I can!" Angelique nodded at him eagerly. "I will help you with the design, Daniel. You will have to do the actual building – you have bigger paws. Have you any paper?" she asked hopefully.

Dan and Sophie shook their heads.

"None at all," Dan said. "Um. I have got lots at home, though. I could go and get some. Or..." He glanced sideways at Sophie, as though he wasn't sure if he was doing the right thing. "Would you like to come home with us?" he added, all in a rush. Then he looked rather embarrassed.

"Oooh, yes, definitely!" Josephine agreed, bouncing up and down. She caught Angelique's eye. "I mean, what a very kind invitation, we would be delighted to accept." She elbowed Angelique in the side. "Wouldn't we?"

"Well, it is rather risky, but then I

would quite like to see inside a human house..." Angelique admitted. "I've never left the gardens before."

"It's actually an apartment, not a house," Sophie put in quickly. "But it's on the top floor, so there's a beautiful view."

"Is there a lift?" Angelique asked, clasping her paws together hopefully. "I've watched the cable car that takes the tourists to the top of the hill for hours and hours. I would *so* much like to see a lift!"

Dan shook his head apologetically. "Just stairs. Lots of them. Mum says she's fitter than she's ever been. But we do have a very fancy coffee machine," he added, giving Angelique a hopeful look. "It does steam for cappuccinos and everything."

"Hmmm." Angelique nodded. "I think that would be very useful for me to see, don't you, Josephine? For the sake of research?"

"Very, *very* useful." Josephine nodded seriously, but her eyes were sparkling.

Angelique suddenly leaned over and hugged Josephine. "I was wrong. I shouldn't have told you off for talking to them," she admitted, hanging her head.

"I told you," Josephine said, a little

smugly. But she hugged her sister back anyway.

Sophie watched the two of them squeaking lovingly at each other and smiled delightedly at Dan. Then she shrugged out of her hoodie and laid it on the stone balustrade. "I think we'll have to disguise you for the walk back," she explained. "Would you mind being wrapped in this?"

The two guinea pigs scrambled in and Sophie snuggled them up in her arms. "Come on, Dan."

"Yes!" Angelique popped her nose out of the hoodie. "Take us back to your apartment – we have a great deal to do!"

CHAPTER SIX

"You have so many books." Angelique sighed, standing in the middle of Dan's room and slowly twirling around. "Shelves and shelves of them!"

Sophie had been worried that someone would spot them on the walk back to the house, but no one had noticed the bright eyes and wobbling whiskers sticking out of her hoodie. They'd hurried up the stairs to the apartment, and now they were showing Angelique and Josephine everything.

"I haven't actually read all of those," Dan admitted, looking a bit embarrassed. "Some of them my mum got for me and I wasn't that keen..." His voice trailed away as he caught the shocked expression on the white guinea pig's face. "I definitely will though," he added quickly. "Would you like to borrow any?"

Angelique's whiskers trembled with excitement and she clasped her paws together. "Yes! I'm sure this one would fit through our door," she murmured, peering up at the shelves. "And this one, and this…"

"That book is larger than your bedroom," Josephine pointed out.

"Anyway, I thought you were supposed to be designing a catapult?"

"I've got a sketchbook here." Dan pulled a large sketchbook off his desk and laid it on the floor in front of Angelique. "Oh, and a book about the Romans. There might be pictures of catapults inside." He pulled a huge book off the shelf and put it next to the sketchbook.

Angelique was actually hopping from paw to paw in excitement. "Oh, look at it, look at it, all those lovely words." She crouched in front of the book and flicked through the pages in a blur of paws. "Yes! Here, Daniel, look. Roman siege engines — that means machines for fighting with. Hmmm." She looked up at Dan thoughtfully. "Do you think that your teacher would let us fire balls of flame?"

"No." Dan shook his head regretfully. "Monsieur Carle's a bit strict. That's why I'd really like my project to be good."

"A pity." Angelique sighed, picking up a pencil that was almost as tall as she was, and starting to scribble madly on the drawing pad. "But never mind. I require sticks, string and a great many elastic bands."

Sophie and Dan ran all over the apartment, finding Angelique the things

she needed. It was actually lucky that
Mum was hard at work on her article,
Sophie realized. It meant there was no
chance of her spotting the guinea pigs.
Especially as Josephine was exploring
the kitchen, *ooh*ing and *aah*ing at the

cupboards full of food and admiring the shiny pans hanging from the ceiling. Sophie caught the ginger-and-white guinea pig climbing into one of the cupboards as she hurried by with an armful of sticks that Dad had been keeping to light the wood-burner.

"I'm just looking!" Josephine said airily, sticking her paw behind the cereal box. Sophie pretended not to notice that the box had a neat little hole chewed in the side.

"Come and see the catapult," Sophie said, holding out her hands for Josephine to step into. "It's amazing – I think it's nearly finished!"

Back in Dan's room, Angelique and Dan were admiring their work. "Look! We're just fitting on the wheels," Dan said excitedly to Sophie.

The main frame of the catapult was ready, built on to the box for some very posh pasta that Mum had bought. Dan had picked up some sticks on the way home and they had Dad's kindling wood too, neatly lashed together to make two tall triangles and a bar across the top. The elastic bands that Sophie had found in the kitchen drawer were trailing down from the cross bar. Sophie frowned, trying to see how it would work. She didn't want to admit to Dan and Angelique that she didn't understand.

Josephine peered at the machine. "What does this do?" she asked, twitching at a piece of string.

"Don't pull that! It's not ready!" Angelique squeaked. "That fires the catapult."

Josephine dropped the string hurriedly and Angelique looped it up out of the way. "It stretches out the elastic, so then when you let go the elastic pings back and makes the catapult arm fly up."

"Those are very good knots holding it all together," Sophie said, peering at them and looking impressed. "I didn't know you could do that, Dan."

"Angelique read that book on knots that Grandpa gave me."

"Why didn't you use those sticks?" Josephine asked, pointing to a small pile left on the floor. "They're very nice and straight."

"We're saving those ones to put the wheels on," Dan explained. "That's why we've built it on a box, you see. So we can put holes in the sides and push the sticks through. Then we put the wheels on the end of the sticks. Those are the bottle tops."

Angelique made a *pppffft* noise and

politely spat shreds of brown plastic out from between her teeth. Then she handed a bottle top to Dan, with a neat, stick-sized hole chewed in the middle. "There! The last one."

"Good thing you like chocolate milk," Sophie said. "You don't even need to paint them." She watched admiringly as Dan and Angelique slid the bottle tops on to the wheel-shaft sticks and Josephine helped Angelique to squeeze glue around the holes.

Then she stood there, tapping a hind paw on the wooden floor. "OH! I cannot wait any longer for this glue to dry! I want to try it now!"

"I know. . ." Angelique nodded. "It's almost dry. We could just help it a little, don't you think?" She glanced around guiltily, and then closed her eyes and clapped her paws together. There was a fizzing noise and the gloopy white glue turned clear and set. "*Ahem*. Very good, quick-drying glue," she murmured, winking at Dan, who stared back at her, wide-eyed. "Now help me pull it along," she said, beckoning to Josephine. "We must make sure it runs smoothly."

They grasped the string attached to the front of the catapult in their tiny paws and hauled, giggling as the heavy machine rolled along behind them.

"It goes! It goes!" squeaked Josephine, as they dragged it out into the passageway.

"Are you two all right?" Mum called from her little office. "Did you want a snack? Sorry I've been so busy, I had to get that work finished."

"She's coming!" Sophie whispered, looking around frantically for guinea pig hiding places. Angelique and Josephine were right next to her bedroom door – they darted inside, dragging the catapult after them. Sophie followed them, hissing, "Under the bed!"

"I can't! I'm all tangled in the string!" Josephine wailed and Sophie crouched down to help her.

"Are you all right, Sophie? I heard a funny noise..."

Sophie turned back to the door, staring at her mum, wide-eyed. Dan was behind her, peering round Mum's arm with a horrified expression on his face.

"Oh!" Mum let out a yelp of amazement, and Sophie closed her eyes. She'd seen them!

"Dan, is that your project? Oh, aren't you clever! It's so good!"

"What. . . Um, yes!" Dan nodded, smiling with relief, and Sophie turned to stare at the catapult.

"Sophie, love, you really do need to tidy up your room," Mum said, frowning a little. "Look at those soft toys lying on the floor."

Sophie bit her lip so as not to laugh. She was sure Josephine was trying not to giggle too – the ginger-and-white furry guinea pig flopped on the floor was definitely wobbling a bit. Angelique was trying so hard to keep still that she was holding her breath and turning pink again. Sophie just hoped Mum wouldn't notice.

"That's such a good model, Dan. I'm really impressed." Mum sighed, and stretched. "I suppose I'd better go and make some dinner. Do you want to go and buy some ice cream for afterwards? You definitely deserve it." She headed out of the room.

Sophie let out a shaky breath. "You're so

clever," she whispered to the guinea pigs. "She absolutely believed you were toys!"

Angelique sat up cautiously. "Has she gone?"

"Yes." Dan peered round the door. "She's in the kitchen."

"Good. Because I've just thought – what are you going to fire out of your catapult?"

"Marbles?" Dan suggested.

Angelique shook her head. "Too dangerous." She marched back into Dan's room to look at their designs, the catapult trundling after her. "Something round, yes..." she murmured. "But quite soft, in case you injure one of your classmates..." She looked up triumphantly. "I have it! Macarons!"

"What?" Dan, Sophie and Josephine all stared at her.

"You should fire macarons, they'd be perfect. Those chocolate ones, then they'd even look like rocks."

"No!" Josephine squeaked in horror. "You can't possibly. What a waste! They'd be smashed to smithereens – all that lovely chocolatey goo!"

Dan looked thoughtful. "Actually, I think Josephine's right," he admitted. "Too messy."

"Quite soft – but not soft enough to fall apart," Josephine muttered, tapping her paws thoughtfully against her cheeks. "Marshmallows! I don't mind if you use those, I don't like them. Much. And I just happened to notice that you had a bag of them in the kitchen cupboard."

"Yes!" Dan raced out to the kitchen and came back with a huge bag of pink and white marshmallows. "We'd better test it fires them OK." He loaded one into the little fabric pouch they'd made and wound back the string pulley. The elastic bands stretched and Sophie held her breath. Angelique watched worriedly, scurrying around the model and hissing with worry whenever it creaked.

Then Dan let go and the marshmallow

flew across the room, hitting the window
with a soft *flumpf*.

"Oh, it's perfect, it works!" Angelique
waved her paws over her head. Dan
cheered. "High five!" He held out his
hand to Angelique
and she stared at
it in surprise for
a second.

Then she patted his hand with her tiny pink paw and giggled.

"I can take it in to school tomorrow," Dan said proudly. "It's *epic*. Monsieur Carle's going to love it. Angelique, you're brilliant."

Angelique stroked the wooden uprights and smiled proudly. "It is indeed *magnifique*," she agreed. "But we have

to go, the others will be wondering where we have got to. Josephine! No more marshmallows!" she added sternly, snatching the bag away from her sister. "We need them! And you'll be sick."

"I'm not eating them!" Josephine said,

through a mouthful of marshmallow.
"I don't even like them. Too fluffy and
sticky." She gave a delicate little burp
behind her paw. "*Pardon*."

Sophie and Dan carried the two guinea
pigs (and a few carefully chosen small
books) back to *Sacré Coeur* in Mum's
shopping bag. It was a nice, breathable
plastic-mesh and Josephine said that being
wrapped up in a dark hoodie would
make her travel-sick – it was absolutely
nothing to do with marshmallows.

Back at the steps at the foot of the
hill, they laid the bag down so the two
guinea pigs could climb out. Sophie
kissed her fingers and patted the top of

Josephine's head. "We should go. We'll come and see you tomorrow, if we can." She looked anxiously at Angelique, who was sitting on the grass, brushing her sleek fur with her paws. She still wasn't quite sure if Angelique was their friend or not. What if she went all grumpy again?

"Oh... Well, yes." The white guinea pig blushed pale pink. She glanced shyly at Sophie and Dan. "I suppose I might have been wrong to say that guinea pigs and humans can't be friends." And then, so quickly that Sophie almost missed it, Angelique hugged her. Just the quickest little furry clasp of her ankle – and she did the same to Dan. "We might be here. If you were passing. Perhaps."

"She means *of course* we'll be here and *please* come and see us," Josephine said, spinning round on her toes and bowing very low to the children. "Until tomorrow, then! *Au revoir!*"

Have you read...

Read on for a sneak peek!

CHAPTER ONE

Sophie peered out over the view, watching the sunlight sparkle on the windows, and wondering who lived there, under the roofs. She couldn't see her own house from here, or she didn't think she could, anyway. She hadn't lived in Paris for long enough to know.

The city *was* very beautiful, but it still
didn't feel like home. Sophie sighed, and
rested her chin on her hands. She missed
her old house, and her old bedroom, and
her cat, Oscar. Grandma was looking

after him while they lived in Paris, but Sophie was sure that Oscar missed her, almost as much as she missed him.

"What are you looking at?" Dan squashed up next to her, leaning over the stone balcony.

"Just things," Sophie said vaguely. "The view."

"Boring," Dan muttered. "This is taking ages. And I'm hungry." He turned round, holding his tummy in both hands and made a starving face at Sophie. His nose scrunched up like a rabbit's, and Sophie smirked. She crossed her eyes and poked her tongue out at the corner of her mouth to make Dan laugh. After all, even a wonderful view can be boring when you've been looking at it for a *VERY LONG TIME.*

All the people who live in Paris love their city so much, and many of them walk up the steep steps to the church on their wedding days to have their photographs taken next to the wonderful view. But it can take an awful long time to get the photographs right, especially when it's windy and your auntie's wedding dress won't stay still properly.

"Sophie and Dan! Stop making faces like that! You're making Dad giggle, and he's supposed to be taking romantic photos!" Mum glared at them, but Dad rolled his eyes, and stuck his tongue out at Dan. Sophie thought Dad might be a bit bored with the photos as well.

This church was one of Sophie's favourite places in Paris. It was so pretty, and there was the fountain to look at, and all the people. She even liked its name, *Sacré Coeur*, which meant Sacred Heart. Sophie thought it was very special to have a whole church that was all about love. Auntie Lou's wedding had been beautiful too, but Sophie had got up early for Mum to curl her hair and fuss over her dress, and she was tired of having to stand still and smile.

"Go and play," Auntie Lou suggested.

"Go and run around for a bit. You can come back and be in the photos later."

"Later?" Dad moaned. "I thought we'd nearly finished!" But Sophie and Dan were already halfway down the white marble steps, and couldn't hear him.